CHRISTMAS 1995

"It is sublime—it will be heard and remembered a hundred Christmases to come." So wrote the reviewer in a newspaper when *A Christmas Carol* was first published. Well— that remark was penned over one hundred and fifty years ago, so it was not a bad forecast! The book sold out on the first day of publication in 1843, but it has never been out of print since.

Not only has it never been out of print—it has been adapted, revised, retold, reoriginated and modernised more than any other work of English literature. It has appeared in the form of plays, films, musicals, television, cartoons, ballets and even puppet shows. It has been translated into just about every language. Whatever form the story appears in, the power always comes through.

It is hard to analyse why this should be so. What is this little story exactly? Is it a ghost story? A fairy story? An allegory? A parable? A fable? A dream vision? A social document? A melodrama? It is all of these things! But that misses the essential point. It is, above all, a joyous shout of human goodness, kindness, forgiveness, charity and pleasantness. It bubbles with laughter and good humour. Cheerful abundance is given to everyone—from the Ghost of Christmas Present with his turkeys, geese, pigs, long strings of sausages, mince pies, plum puddings, barrels of oysters, chestnuts, apples, oranges, pears, huge cakes and great bowls of punch, down to Mrs. Cratchit's rather small goose and plum pudding.

Because the story is so essentially and intensely human, it comes across the years to us today, as if through a time warp. It is not attached to any date or time. The negative things are, sadly, still with us—poverty, misery, disadvantage, wilful ignorance of the plight of others. But let us hope that the positive things are still with us also—caring, concern, kindness, benevolence, good humour and laughter. May you, in reading this lovely edition of the book, find laughter in your own hearts and spread it abundantly around you.

A Merry Christmas!

David Charles Dickens

David Charles Dickens
Great-Grandson of CHARLES DICKENS

Hand Lettering by Virginia Sembower
Typography by Curt Knupp

A Christmas Carol

By Charles Dickens

(Adapted for modern readers)

Edited by Carol L. Marsh
Illustrated by Gary Head

Hallmark Cards, Inc.

Marley's Ghost

Old Marley was as dead as a doornail. And Scrooge knew it, of course.
Scrooge and he had been partners for many years. Yet Scrooge never painted
out old Marley's name. There it stood, years afterwards, above the warehouse
door—Scrooge and Marley. Sometimes people new to the business called
Scrooge "Scrooge," and sometimes "Marley." He answered to both names. It
didn't matter to him.

Oh, but Ebenezer Scrooge was stingy! He was a squeezing, wrenching,
grasping, clutching old sinner! Nobody ever stopped him in the street to say,
"My dear Scrooge, how are you? When will you come to see me?" No beggars
asked him for money. No children asked him what time it was. In fact, people
seldom talked to him at all. But what did Scrooge care! To be left alone was the
very thing he liked.

One Christmas Eve, old Scrooge sat in his office. It was cold, bleak, foggy
weather. The city clocks had just struck three, but it was quite dark already.

The door of Scrooge's office was open so that he could keep his eye on his
clerk, who sat at a tiny desk in the next room copying letters. Scrooge had a
very small fire, but the clerk's fire was very much smaller. And he couldn't add
more coal, for Scrooge kept the coalbox in his own room, and the clerk knew
that if he came in with the shovel, he would be in danger of losing his job. So
the clerk put on his white scarf and tried to warm himself by the flickering
candle that lighted his work.

"A merry Christmas, Uncle! God bless you!" cried a cheerful voice. It was
Scrooge's nephew who came in just then.

"Bah!" said Scrooge. "Humbug!"

"Christmas a humbug, Uncle? You don't mean that!"

"I do. Away with Merry Christmas! What's Christmastime to you but a time
for paying bills without money—a time for finding yourself a year older and not
an hour richer. If I had my way, every idiot who goes around with 'Merry
Christmas' on his lips would be boiled in his own soup and buried with a stake
of holly through his heart. He should!"

"Bah!" said Scrooge. "Humbug!"

"Uncle!"

"Nephew, keep Christmas in your own way, and let me keep it in mine."

"Keep it? But you don't keep it!"

"Let me leave it alone, then. It's my business, Nephew, not yours!"

"Don't be angry, Uncle. Come! Have dinner with us tomorrow."

Scrooge said that he would not, and he said it most rudely.

"But why?" cried Scrooge's nephew. "Why?"

"Good afternoon!"

"But, Uncle, you never come to see my wife and me!"

"Good afternoon."

"I want nothing from you; I ask nothing of you—why can't we be friends?"

"Good afternoon."

"I am sorry to find you so stubborn. But I have never quarreled with you, and I'll keep my Christmas humor to the last. So a merry Christmas, Uncle!"

At closing time Scrooge climbed down from his stool. When the clerk saw him, he quickly snuffed his candle out and put on his hat.

"You want all day off tomorrow, I suppose?"

"If it's all right, sir."

"It's not all right, and it's not fair. If I stopped a day's pay for it, you'd think it was unfair, wouldn't you?"

"Yes, sir."

"And yet you don't think it unfair when I pay a day's wages for no work."

"It's only once a year, sir."

"A poor excuse for picking a man's pocket every twenty-fifth of December! Well, be here all the earlier next morning."

The clerk promised that he would, and Scrooge walked out with a growl. The office was closed in a twinkling. The clerk had no topcoat, so he wrapped the long ends of his white scarf around him and ran home as fast as he could to play with his children.

...he wrapped the long ends of his white scarf around him and ran home as fast as he could...

Scrooge ate his lonely dinner in his usual lonely restaurant. Then he read the newspapers and went home to bed. He lived in a towering building that once belonged to his partner. The building was old and gloomy now, for nobody lived in it but Scrooge.

As he started to unlock the door, Scrooge looked at the knocker that hung on it, and there he saw not a knocker but Marley's face. It was not angry but looked at Scrooge as Marley used to look—ghostly glasses turned up upon its ghostly forehead.

As Scrooge stared at the face, which had a greenish light about it, it changed back into a knocker again. He said "Pooh, pooh!" and closed the door with a bang. The sound boomed through the house like thunder. Every room seemed to have an echo of its own. Scrooge was not a man to be frightened by echoes. He locked the door, walked across the hall, and climbed the stairs.

Up Scrooge went, not caring about how dark it was. Darkness is cheap, and Scrooge liked it. But he still remembered the face on the knocker, and before he shut his door, he walked through his rooms to see that everything was all right.

Quite satisfied, he locked and double-locked his door. Then he undressed, put on his nightgown, slippers and nightcap, and sat down to rest before the low fire.

Suddenly he heard a clanking noise far down below as if someone were dragging a heavy chain over the cellar floor.

The noise grew much louder and seemed to come from the rooms below; then it came up the stairs and headed straight toward his door.

It came on through the heavy door, and a spirit passed into the room before his eyes. The tiny flame in the fireplace burned brighter, as though it cried, "I know him! Marley's ghost!"

And, indeed, it was Marley, in his pigtail, usual short coat, tights, and boots. His body was so clear that Scrooge could look right through him and see the two buttons on his coat behind. But though he looked at the ghost and noticed the folded handkerchief wrapped around its head and chin, he still didn't believe it was real.

The tiny flame in the fireplace burned brighter, as though it cried, "I know him! Marley's ghost!"

"Well, now!" said Scrooge, as cold as ever. "What do you want with me?"

"Much!" It was Marley's voice—no doubt about it.

"Who are you?"

"Ask me who I was."

"Who were you, then?"

"In life I was your partner, Jacob Marley."

"Humbug!"

"You don't believe in me?"

"I don't."

"You see me, don't you?"

"Yes."

"Why do you doubt your senses?"

"Because something must be bothering them. A slight disorder of the stomach makes them cheat. You may be an undigested bit of beef, a blot of mustard, a crumb of cheese, a piece of underdone potato. There's more of gravy than of grave about you, whatever you are!"

Scrooge was not in the habit of cracking jokes, nor did he really feel very funny then. The truth is that he was trying to keep Marley from seeing how frightened he was.

But he was frightened much worse when the phantom took the bandage off its head, as if it were too warm to wear indoors, and its lower jaw dropped down upon its breast!

"Mercy! Awful spirit, why do you trouble me? Why do you walk the earth, and why do you come to me?"

"I cannot tell you all I would. I cannot rest—I cannot stay—I cannot linger anywhere. In life I had no time for anything but our business. Hear me! In life my thoughts never left the narrow limits of our office. Now, in death, I must travel far to make up for all the things I should have done. Weary journeys lie before me!"

"Dead for seven years. And traveling all the time! You travel fast?"

"On the wings of the wind."

"But you were always a good man of business, Jacob," Scrooge said.

"Business!" cried the ghost, wringing its hands again. "Mankind was my business. Love for others was my business. Charity and mercy were my business."

Scrooge was so upset to hear the spirit going on like this that he began to shake.

"Hear me! My time is nearly gone."

"I will. But don't be hard on me, Jacob!"

"I am here to warn you that you still have a chance to escape my fate, Ebenezer. You will be haunted by three spirits."

"Is that the chance you mentioned, Jacob? I—I think I'd rather not."

"Without their visits you cannot hope to avoid the path I walk. Expect the first tonight, when the bell tolls one. You will see me no more, but be sure, for your own sake, that you remember what I have told you!"

The spirit walked backward from him, and at every step the window raised itself a little, so when the spirit reached it, it was wide open.

Scrooge closed the window and examined the door. It was still double-locked. He tried to say "Humbug!" but couldn't quite get it out. Instead he went straight to bed, pulled up the cover, and fell asleep immediately.

The First of the Three Spirits

When Scrooge awoke, it was dark. But as he lay there, he heard a church clock strike ONE.

Light flashed up in the room, and the curtains of his bed were pulled aside by a strange figure. Its hair, which hung far down its back, was white like an old man's, and yet the face was smooth like a child's. It held a branch of fresh green holly in its hand, and its clothes were trimmed with summer flowers.

"Are you the spirit, sir, I was told to expect?"

"I am!"

"Who and what are you?"

"I am the Ghost of Christmas Past."

"Long past?"

"No. Your past. We will see shadows of the things that have been, but they will not be able to see or hear us. Rise and walk with me!"

Scrooge wanted to say that the hour was late, the bed was warm, the weather was bitter; that he was dressed only in his slippers, nightgown, and nightcap; and that he had a bad cold. But he didn't think it would do any good. Instead, he climbed out of bed and followed the spirit until it moved toward the window. Then Scrooge became more frightened than ever.

"I am only a man. I'll fall!"

"Touch my hand there," said the spirit, laying it upon his heart. As the words were spoken, they passed through the wall and stood on the sidewalk of a busy city. It was plain by the decorations in the shop windows that here, too, it was Christmastime. The ghost stopped at a certain warehouse door and asked Scrooge if he knew it.

"Know it! I once worked here!"

"I am the Ghost of Christmas Past."

They went in. There was an old gentleman sitting behind such a high desk that if he had been two inches taller, he would have knocked his head against the ceiling. Scrooge cried in excitement, "Why, it's old Fezziwig!"

Old Fezziwig laid down his pen and looked up at the clock. He rubbed his hands, adjusted his waistcoat, laughed all over himself from his shoes to his belly, and called out in a jolly voice: "Yo ho, there! Ebenezer! Dick!"

A young man, who was Scrooge's former self, hurried into the room with another young man.

"Dick Wilkins!" said Scrooge to the ghost. "My old fellow worker. Dear, dear!"

"Yo ho, my boys!" said Fezziwig. "No more work tonight. Christmas Eve, Dick. Christmas, Ebenezer! Let's have the shades up before a man can say Jack Robinson! Clear away, my lads, and let's have lots of room here!"

Clear away! There was nothing they wouldn't have cleared away for old Fezziwig. Everything movable was packed off, the floor was swept, the lamps were turned up, coal was heaped upon the fire, and the warehouse was as snug and warm and dry and bright a ballroom as you could hope to see on a winter's night.

In came a fiddler with a music book, and he sat at the tall desk. In came Mrs. Fezziwig, smiling happily. In came the three Miss Fezziwigs. In came their boyfriends. In came all the young men and women who worked for Fezziwig. In came the housemaid with her cousin the baker. In came the cook with her friend the milkman. In they all came, one after another, and away they all danced, down the floor and back again, round and round as the fiddler played. At last old Fezziwig clapped his hands to stop the dance and cried out "Well done!" The fiddler dried his face and had a cool drink while everyone talked and laughed at once.

Then there were more dances, and there were cake and eggnog and cold roast beef and mince pies and plenty to drink. It was a happy evening, and everyone danced and ate and laughed to his heart's content.

When the clock struck eleven, the ball broke up. Mr. and Mrs. Fezziwig stood by the door and, shaking hands with every person as he or she went out, wished each a merry Christmas. When everybody had gone but Ebenezer and Dick, they did the same to them, and the lads then went to their beds, which were under a counter in the back shop.

"A small matter," said the ghost, "to make these silly folks so happy. He really hasn't spent much money."

"It isn't that," said Scrooge, still speaking like his former self. "He has the power to make us happy or unhappy, to make our jobs easier or harder. His power lies in being kind and thoughtful and doing nice things for all who work for him. So you see, the happiness he gives is just as great as if it cost a fortune."

Suddenly he became very tired and found himself back in his own bedroom. He stumbled into bed and immediately sank into a heavy sleep.

In they all came, one after another, and away they all danced...

The Second of the Three Spirits

Scrooge awoke in his own bedroom. There was no doubt about that. But there was a great light coming from his sitting room. He put on his slippers and timidly shuffled in to see what was causing it. The walls and ceiling were so hung with green branches that it looked like a forest, and the merriest blaze roared up the chimney that the old fireplace had known for many and many a winter. Heaped upon the floor to form a kind of throne were turkeys, geese, pigs, long strings of sausages, mince pies, plum puddings, barrels of oysters, chestnuts, apples, oranges, pears, huge cakes, and great bowls of punch. Upon this throne sat a smiling giant who held a glowing torch raised high to shed its light on Scrooge as he came peeping round the door.

"Come in—come in and know me better, man! I am the Ghost of Christmas Present. Look at me! You have never seen anyone like me before."

"Never! Spirit, take me where you will. I am ready to learn what you will teach me."

"Touch my robe!"

Scrooge did as he was told. The room and its contents all vanished, and they stood before the house of Scrooge's clerk, Bob Cratchit, on a snowy Christmas morning.

Mrs. Cratchit was dressed poorly in a patched-up gown, but in her hair she wore bright ribbons. She set the table, helped by Belinda Cratchit, second of her daughters, who also wore ribbons in her hair. Master Peter Cratchit wore one of his father's shirts, which was much too large for him. And now two smaller Cratchits, boy and girl, came tearing in, screaming that outside the baker's they had smelled the goose, their very own goose! These young Cratchits danced about the table and shouted happily while Peter Cratchit blew the fire under the pan until the potatoes, bubbling up, knocked loudly at the lid to be let out and peeled.

"What is keeping your precious father?" said Mrs. Cratchit. "And your brother, Tiny Tim! And Martha!"

"Here's Martha, Mother!" said a girl who was watching out the window.

"Here's Martha, Mother!" cried the two young Cratchits. "Hurrah! There's such a goose, Martha!"

"Why, bless your heart, my dear. How late you are!" said Mrs. Cratchit, kissing her a dozen times and taking off her coat and bonnet for her. "But never mind. Now you're here. Sit down before the fire, my dear, and have a warm drink."

He put on his slippers and timidly shuffled in to see what was causing it.

"No, no! There's Father coming," cried the two young Cratchits, who were everywhere at once. "Hide, Martha, hide!"

So Martha hid herself, and in came Bob, the father, with at least three feet of scarf wrapped around him, and his threadbare clothes patched and brushed. Tiny Tim was perched upon his shoulder. Poor Tiny Tim. He held a little crutch, and on his legs he wore an iron brace!

"Why, where's our Martha?" cried Bob Cratchit, looking round.

"Not coming," said Mrs. Cratchit.

"Not coming?" said Bob, suddenly looking very sad. "Not coming on Christmas Day?" Then Martha popped out from behind the closet door and ran into his arms, while the two young Cratchits carried Tiny Tim off into the kitchen so that he could hear the pudding bubbling in the pan.

"And how did little Tim behave?" asked Mrs. Cratchit when Bob had hugged his daughter to his heart's content.

"As good as gold," said Bob. "Somehow he gets thoughtful, sitting by himself so much. He told me that he hoped people saw him in church because he was a cripple and it might be pleasant for them to remember on Christmas Day who made cripples walk and blind men see."

Before another word was spoken, Tiny Tim was brought back by his brother and sister to his stool beside the fire. Bob mixed hot punch, stirred it round and round, and put it by the fire to simmer. Master Peter and the two young Cratchits went after the goose, and they soon returned with it, held high for all to see.

Mrs. Cratchit made the gravy hissing hot. Master Peter mashed the potatoes, Miss Belinda sweetened up the applesauce, Martha dusted the plates, and Bob put Tiny Tim beside him at a corner of the table. The two young Cratchits set chairs for everybody; then they scrambled onto their seats and crammed spoons into their mouths to keep from shrieking for goose before their turns came to be served. At last everything was ready, and grace was said. There was a breathless pause as Mrs. Cratchit looked slowly along the carving knife and prepared to plunge it into the goose. But when she did, and when the long expected gush of stuffing popped forth, they all began to talk at once, and even Tiny Tim, excited by the two young Cratchits, beat on the table with the handle of his knife, and feebly cried, "Hurrah!"

Bob said he didn't believe there ever was such a goose cooked. Everyone bragged on its tenderness and flavor and size. Indeed, with the applesauce and mashed potatoes, there was enough dinner for the whole family. Mrs. Cratchit looked at one small bite left upon the dish and said with great delight that they hadn't eaten it all, at last! But now the plates were changed by Miss Belinda,

"...There's Father coming," cried the two young Cratchits, who were everywhere at once.

and Mrs. Cratchit left the room to bring in the pudding. In half a minute she proudly entered with the pudding, as firm as a speckled cannon ball, blazing in a tiny measure of brandy and crowned with holly.

"Oh, what a wonderful pudding!" Bob Cratchit said. Everybody had something to say about it, but nobody said or thought it was at all a small pudding for a large family. Any Cratchit would have blushed to hint at such a thing.

At last the dinner was all done, the table was cleared, and the hearth swept. Apples and oranges were put upon the table and a shovelful of chestnuts on the fire.

Then all the Cratchit family sat around the hearth, and Bob Cratchit served the punch with beaming looks while the chestnuts on the fire spluttered noisily. Then Bob proposed, "A merry Christmas to us all, my dears. God bless us!" Which all the family repeated.

"God bless us every one!" said Tiny Tim, the last of all. He sat very close to his father's side upon his small stool. Bob held his withered little hand in his as if he dreaded that Tiny Tim might be taken from him.

"Mr. Scrooge!" said Bob. "A toast to Mr. Scrooge!"

Scrooge was surprised to hear his own name.

"Mr. Scrooge, indeed!" cried Mrs. Cratchit. "I wish I had him here. I'd give him a piece of my mind!"

"My dear," said Bob, "the children! Christmas Day!"

"I'll drink it for your sake and the day's," said Mrs. Cratchit, "not for his. Long life to him! A merry Christmas and a happy New Year! He'll be very merry and very happy, I'm sure!"

The children drank the toast after her, but they only did it to please their father. Tiny Tim drank it last of all. The mention of Scrooge had cast a dark shadow on the party which lasted for a full five minutes.

After it had passed away, they were ten times merrier than before. All this time the chestnuts and the jug of punch went round and round. After a while they had a song from Tiny Tim about a lost child traveling in the snow. He had a clear little voice and sang it very well, indeed. There was nothing special about all this. They were not a handsome family—they were not well dressed, their shoes were scuffed, their clothes were scanty. But they were happy and grateful and pleased with one another, and when the room began to fade away, Scrooge had his eye on Tiny Tim until the last.

It surprised Scrooge, as this scene disappeared, to hear a hearty laugh. It was a much greater surprise to recognize it as his own nephew's and to find himself in a bright room of his nephew's house with the spirit by his side.

When Scrooge's nephew laughed, his wife laughed, too, and they were both joined by their guests, who sat around the table with them.

"He said that Christmas was a humbug!" cried Scrooge's nephew. "He believed it, too!"

Again they all laughed. "He's a funny old fellow," Scrooge's nephew went on. "He's not as pleasant as he should be, but I have nothing to say against him. He hurts no one but himself. Here he takes it into his head to dislike us, and he won't come to eat with us. So what happens? He misses a fine dinner."

Everybody agreed that the dinner had been perfect, and they all laughed again at Scrooge for having turned down the chance to share it.

After tea they had some music. They were a happy group who loved to sing—especially Topper, who could growl away in a bass voice and never even get red in the face over it.

But they didn't spend the whole evening singing. After a while they played games, for it is good to be children sometimes, especially at Christmas.

"Look," whispered Scrooge, "they're starting. Let's stay a bit longer, Spirit!"

It was a game called "Yes and No," where Scrooge's nephew had to think of something and the rest must find out what. And he could only answer their questions by a "yes" or a "no." By his answers they learned that he was thinking of an animal, a live animal, rather a disagreeable animal, an animal that growled and grunted sometimes and talked sometimes and lived in London and walked about the streets and wasn't paid much attention and wasn't led by anybody and didn't live in a zoo and was never killed by a butcher and was not a horse or a donkey or a cow or a bull or a tiger or a dog or a pig or a cat or a bear. At every new question asked him, the nephew burst into a fresh roar of laughter and became so tickled that he had to get up off the sofa and stamp his foot. At last the plump sister cried out, "I know what it is, Fred! I know what it is!"

"What is it?" cried Fred.

"It's your Uncle Scro-o-o-o-oge!"

Which it certainly was. Everyone laughed and said it had been a fine game. But some of them thought that the reply to "Is it a bear?" ought to have been "Yes."

Suddenly the whole scene changed again, and Scrooge and the spirit were once more upon their travels.

As they stood together in an open place, a church bell rang. Scrooge looked about him for the ghost, but it was gone. He remembered that Jacob Marley had said there would be a third ghost, and lifting up his eyes, he saw a phantom whose face was hidden by a dark hood coming across the ground toward him.

The phantom moved slowly and silently.

The Last of the Spirits

The phantom moved slowly and silently. When it came near him, Scrooge bent down upon his knee, for this spirit seemed so sad that Scrooge was frightened. Wrapped around it was a long black robe which covered its head, its face, its body, and left nothing of it visible except one outstretched hand. The spirit neither spoke nor moved.

"Are you the Ghost of Christmas Yet to Come? Ghost of the future! I am more afraid of you than of any spirit I have seen. But I know that you've come to do me good, and I hope to live to be a better man than what I was, so I am ready to go with you gladly. Will you not speak to me?"

It remained silent. The hand was pointed straight before them.

"Lead on! Lead on! The night is almost gone, and we must not lose a moment, I know. Lead on, Spirit!"

They were immediately standing in the heart of the city on Commercial Street, among the merchants. The spirit stopped beside one little group of businessmen. The hand was pointed to them, so Scrooge walked forward to listen to their talk.

"No," said a great fat man with a monstrous chin, "I don't know much about it either way. I only know he's dead."

"When did he die?" asked another.

"Last night, I believe."

"Why, what was the matter with him? I thought he'd never die."

"God knows," said the first with a yawn.

"What has he done with his money?" asked a red-faced gentleman.

"I haven't heard," said the man with the large chin. "His company, perhaps. He hasn't left it to me. That's all I know."

Scrooge was surprised that the spirit should want him to listen to something so unimportant. But he was certain that it must have some hidden purpose. He wondered what it might be. It could have nothing to do with the death of Jacob, his old partner, for that was past, and this was the ghost of the future.

He looked about for himself, but though the clock pointed to his usual time of day for being there, he could not see himself among the crowds that walked up and down the street. This didn't surprise Scrooge, however, for he had already made up his mind to change his way of life. He supposed this to be the reason for his not being in his old place at this hour.

They left the busy street and went into another part of town to a shop where iron, rags, bottles, bones, and greasy rubbish were bought. An old grey-haired rascal sat smoking his pipe by the doorway. Scrooge and the phantom arrived just as a woman with a heavy bundle slunk into the shop. She had scarcely entered when another woman also carrying a bundle came in too, and she was closely followed by a man who brought a bundle of his own. When each one saw the other two there, they all three burst into a laugh.

"Let the scrubwoman be first!" cried she who had entered first. "Let the washerwoman be second, and let the undertaker's man be the third. Look here, old Joe. Ain't this a joke! If we haven't all three met here without meaning to!"

"You couldn't have met in a better place. You all come here often enough. What have you to sell? What have you got to sell?"

"Wait a minute, Joe, and you shall see."

Joe went down on his knees to make it easier to open the bundle and dragged out a large, heavy roll of some dark stuff.

"What are these? Ah! Bed curtains!"

"Yes! Bed curtains! Don't drop that oil upon the blankets, now."

"His blankets?"

"Whose else's do you think? He isn't likely to catch a cold without 'em, I dare say. If he wanted to keep 'em after he was dead, the wicked old sinner, why wasn't he a better man in his lifetime? If he had been, he'd have had somebody to look after him when he died instead of lying gasping out his last breath there, alone by himself. Ah! You can look through that shirt till your eyes ache, but you won't find a hole in it or a threadbare place. It's the best he had, and a fine one, too. They'd have wasted it by dressing him in it if it hadn't been for me."

When each one saw the other two there, they all three burst into a laugh.

Scrooge listened in fear.

"Spirit! I see, I see. What has happened to this unhappy man might happen to me! My life leads that way now. Merciful heaven, what is this?"

The scene had changed, and now he almost touched a bare, uncurtained bed. Pale moonlight fell upon this bed, and on it, unwatched and uncared for, was the body of the robbed, unknown man.

Just as suddenly, the scene changed once more. The ghost conducted him to poor Bob Cratchit's house—where he had visited before—and they found the mother and children seated around the fire.

The mother laid her sewing upon the table and put her hand up to her face. "The color hurts my eyes," she said. "They're better again now. The candlelight makes them water, and I wouldn't show red eyes to your father when he comes home for the world. It must be nearly time for him now."

"Past it," Peter answered. "But I think he has walked a little slower than he used to these last few evenings, Mother."

"I have known him to walk with—I have known him to walk with Tiny Tim upon his shoulder very fast, indeed."

"And so have I," cried Peter. "Often."

"And so have I," said another. They all had.

"But he was very light to carry, and his father loved him so, that it was no trouble—no trouble. But hush, now, there is your father at the door!"

She hurried out to meet him as Bob, in his ragged white scarf, came in. His tea was ready for him by the fire, and they all tried to be first to help him to it. Then the two young Cratchits got upon his knees, and each child laid a little cheek against his face as if to say, "Don't mind it, Father. Don't be sad!"

Bob acted very cheerful with them and spoke pleasantly to all the family. He looked at the new suit upon the table and praised the work and speed of Mrs. Cratchit and the girls. It would be ready in time for Tiny Tim to be buried in on Sunday, he said.

"Sunday! Then you went to the cemetery today, Robert?"

"Yes, my dear," he said. "I wish you could have gone. It would have done you good to see how green a place it is. But you'll see it often. I promised him that I would walk there on Sundays. My little, little child! My little child!"

He broke down all at once. He couldn't help it. He had loved Tiny Tim so!

"Spirit," said Scrooge, "something tells me that our visit is nearly over. Tell me who that man was with the covered face whom we saw lying dead."

The Ghost of Christmas Yet to Come took him to a deserted graveyard.

The spirit stood among the graves and pointed down to one.

"Before I move closer to that headstone to which you point, answer me one question. Are you showing me the things that will be or are they only the things that may be?"

Still the ghost pointed downward to the grave by which it stood.

"A man's life may lead him down unhappy paths. But if he changes his life and becomes a better man, then he might have time to find happier paths to follow. Isn't that so, Spirit?"

The spirit was as silent as ever.

Scrooge crept towards it, trembling as he went. Following the finger, he read upon the stone his own name—Ebenezer Scrooge.

"Am I that man who lay upon the bed? No, Spirit! Oh, no, no! Spirit! hear me! I am not the man I was. Because of this visit, I will never be that man again! Why show me this if I am past all hope? Tell me that by changing my life I may change these things you have shown me!"

For the first time the phantom lowered its hand.

"I will honor Christmas in my heart and try to keep it all the year. I will live in the past, the present, and the future. The spirits of all three shall live within me. I will never forget the lessons that they teach. Oh, tell me I may erase away the writing on this stone!"

As he reached out to touch the dark robe, the phantom began to change. It shrunk, grew thin, and dwindled down into a bedpost.

Yes, and the bedpost was his own. The bed was his own, the room was his own. And, best and happiest of all, there was still time left for him to change his life!

Outside, the church bells were ringing loudly. Running to the window, he opened it and stuck his head out. No fog, no mist, no night. It was a clear, bright, golden day.

"What's today?" cried Scrooge, calling downward to a boy in Sunday clothes.

"Today? Why, Christmas Day!"

"It's Christmas Day! I haven't missed it. Do you know the butcher shop in the next street over at the corner?"

"I sure do."

"An intelligent boy! A very fine boy! Do you know whether they've sold the prize turkey that was hanging up there? Not the little prize turkey—the big one?"

"What, the one as big as me?"

"What a delightful boy! Yes, my boy!"

"It's hanging there now."

"Is it? Go and buy it. Go and tell them to bring it here. I'll tell them where to take it. Come back with the man and I'll give you a shilling. Come back with him in less than five minutes and I'll give you half a crown!"

The boy was off like a shot.

"I'll send it to Bob Cratchit's! He won't know who sent it. It's twice the size of Tiny Tim!"

He wrote down the address and went to open the street door to be ready for the butcher when he came. What a turkey it was! Scrooge had never seen such a bird, and he rubbed his hands with glee as he watched the man taking it to Bob Cratchit's.

Then Scrooge dressed himself in his very best clothes and at last got out into the streets. Walking with his hands behind him, Scrooge greeted everyone he met with a delighted smile. He looked so pleasant that people smiled back and said, "Good morning, sir! A merry Christmas to you!"

And Scrooge often said afterwards that of all the happy sounds he had ever heard, those were the happiest of all.

In the afternoon he walked to his nephew's house.

...Scrooge greeted everyone he met with a delighted smile.

"Is your master at home, my dear?" said Scrooge to the girl who opened the door. "Nice girl! Very."

"Yes, sir."

"Where is he, my love?"

"He's in the dining room, sir, with the mistress."

"He knows me," said Scrooge. "I'll go on in, my dear."

"Fred! There's a gentleman to see you."

"Why, bless my soul!" cried Fred. "It's Uncle Scrooge!"

"I have come to dinner. Will you let me in, Fred?"

Let him in?! Fred shook his hand warmly, and his wife kissed Scrooge on the cheek. He felt at home in five minutes. Nothing could be merrier. His niece looked just the same. So did Topper when he came. So did everyone when they came. Wonderful party, wonderful games, wonderful happiness!

Scrooge was early at the office next morning. If he could only be there first and catch Bob Cratchit coming in late! He had his heart set on it.

And he did it.

The clock struck nine. No Bob. A quarter past. No Bob. Bob was eighteen and a half minutes late. Scrooge sat with his door wide open that he might see him come in.

Bob's hat was off before he opened the door—his scarf, too. He was on his stool in a jiffy, writing away with his pen, trying to make up for those eighteen and a half minutes.

"Hello!" growled Scrooge in his usual voice. "What do you mean by coming here at this time of day?"

"I am very sorry, sir. I know I am late."

"You are? Yes. I think you are. Step this way if you please."

"It's only once a year, sir. It won't happen again. I was making rather merry yesterday, sir."

"Now, I'll tell you what, my friend. I am not going to stand for this sort of thing any longer. And therefore," Scrooge continued, leaping from his stool so that Bob took two steps backward, "and therefore, I am about to raise your salary!"

Bob trembled and got a little nearer to the door.

"A merry Christmas, Bob!" said Scrooge. With a twinkle in his eyes, he clapped him on the back. "A merrier Christmas, Bob, my good fellow, than I have given you for many a year! I'll raise your salary and help your family, and we will talk it over this very afternoon, Bob! Build up the fires, and buy a fresh bucket of coal before you dot another 'i,' Bob Cratchit!"

Some people laughed to see the change in him, but he was happy, and that was enough for him.

Scrooge more than kept his word. He did it all, and much, much more. And to Tiny Tim, who did not die, he was a second father. He became as good a friend, as good a master, and as good a man as the old city had ever known. Some people laughed to see the change in him, but he was happy, and that was enough for him.

Scrooge had no further meetings with spirits, and it was always said of him that he knew how to keep Christmas as well as any man alive. May that be truly said of us, all of us! And so, as Tiny Tim observed:

God Bless Us,
Every One!